OXYMORON

HE WAS CHAOTIC, SHE WAS POETIC

IQRA ANSARI

ISBN 979-888521148-2

The battles

worth winning

are the ones

you fight

inside of you.

Contents

Oxymoron

He Was Chaotic, She Was Poetic

IQRA ANSARI

NOTION PRESS

Preface

Acknowledgements

NOTION PRESS

India. Singapore. Malaysia.

Prologue

Akira is an investment banker struggling to be a novelist and a writer which was her dream since childhood. Through her life she's been very dedicated towards her family and always had her mom as her support.

Her view towards life is different and that makes her unique. A few years back she had broken up with Marvin. They had been together for a long time yet they failed to save their relationship somehow.

She feels like she's too old & cold for this generation where she likes to enjoy the vibes in the world full of physical touch. Even after trying really hard to focus on her writing, her profession always became a hurdle for her.

She has finally quit her job to pursue her passion. Sometimes working on your passion can heal all your wounds.

Did she got over from her past she been thinking holding over connections with?

About The Author

Iqra Ansari is a self-published author. She has been writing for over 8 years, as a hobby, and finally took the leap to self-publish. She has written fiction for years in additional to original contemporary romance and romantic suspense stories.

She is currently working on a stand-alone full length contemporary romance and have started outlining the fantasy romance story.

She love telling stories and creating something that allows people to go on a journey of the mind. She has co-authored anthology like "*The Warrior Heart*", "*Shajar Lafzon Ka*", "*The Hidden Hero*". She is about to publish her second fictional novel, *The Eve*, a different kind of love story.

Special Thanks Abhiraj Das

CHAPTER ONE

I walk in the cafeteria to get myself some coffee, it's 8 in the morning. I know it's too early for a cup of coffee but the aroma of the coffee is the best part of this office or it was. As the aroma of nice mildly roasted coffee beans reaches me and calm myself down from the hype of this day being the last day of my office, I sit down on the chair taking a sip, I remember how I used to tell Marvin how I wanted to run away from this place and start a new life and when the time came, how does leaving feel so heavy. As I took the last sip of the coffee, I told myself it doesn't matter how heavy or difficult it be I have to carry on, if I want to start new, I have to be strong.

I finally decided to lift myself up from the chair and walk out of the half-lit café. As I walk out of the cafeteria the dimmed yellow light which used to give the café a nostalgic relaxing touch now seemed to be familiar and comforting, yet I can't let the comfort hold me back, not when I have made up my mind.

On my way out I tell myself 'Akira no matter what happens no matter what you feel, you can't stop now. You have to achieve your goal; you have to be the Bestselling Novelist.'

After a little pep talk to myself, I reached my desk. As I sit at my work desk with a half-crooked smile and eyes filled with tears, not sure if it was the happiness of starting something new or the sorrow of leaving everything behind.

I took the iPod out of my bag, plugged in my earphone and started to go through the playlist on it. After skipping a few soundtracks, I ended up listening to the 'beating of the heart' by 'beats of Blaine'. The song that I have been listening to ever since Marvin left me. I don't know why this song is so underrated. No one really knows this song and no one really likes it. But on the other hand, I can't get over the lyrics. I close my eyes as the song starts.

Since I've met you, I have become capable
Since I've met you, I've achieved it all
Since I've met you, I've become more of myself.
Since I've met you, I started living whole.
Your abode is with me,
Looking for your lane, I found my house
You hold the meaning to my life.
Looking for you I finally found my lord.
For world I am just a human,
For you, I am a poetry.
& that's what I always wanted to be
& With you I forget all my misery.

as the music stops, I lift my head up. Staring at oblivion and remembering the lyrics, 'this is what love feels like, maybe this is the kind of love I have been looking for all along.'

As I was trying to drag myself out from the depth of the lyrics. I heard a familiar voice from behind calling for me. 'Can I get the access card for the main gate?' he said. Though the voice was familiar and he had asked me the same question like a million times by now, who so ever this guy is he never fails to annoy me, I always felt like punching his face when he ask for the access card, but this time it was different. His voice felt a bit heavy. It felt like he wanted to say more but was holding back. In a split second I was pulled out of the fantasy world of perfect love to the reality where this annoying guy can't even carry his own access card. Just like always my answer is the same. Short and precise 'No.' trying to contain my anger. He always annoys me for this. But somehow this time it was a little different. He sounded different. Maybe I'm just being stupid.

Before I could react to him, my colleague Valerie walked in.

"Hey, Akira, you're here, you have to attend the goodbye formalities and the speech, hope you're ready?", Valerie said with a grim smile on her face. She knew that I hated these formalities and goodbye speeches. But she never misses an opportunity to mock me, though it is irritating but I'll miss it. I just gave her a smile and we went out to take a short walk which she insisted I should go.I kept the iPod on the desk and went along with her.

As we walked back in the office, I was greeted with a goodbye cake. I don't understand why. I mean though I will be leaving the office but I will be in the same town. Anyhow I can't disappoint my colleagues as they have always been supportive to me.

I stood in front of everyone. It wasn't the whole office staff, just people whom I have worked with. I stood and started saying my last words in this office,

"It feels great to see you all here. During my tenure in this company, I have witnessed how loaded you people stay with your work, thank you so much for taking out time for me."

I took a pause, not able to understand what to say next. I looked at Valerie and remembered our days in this office. How she always has been there with me. Whenever I had any doubts she has always helped me solving up my problems. Irrespective of her own loads she has never refused to support me.

"It is a situation of mixed feelings for me. We have worked together for so long but now the time to bid goodbye has arrived."

I could see tears in her eyes, as I spoke. I honestly didn't know that we shared this bond together.

"Standing here, I feel that I have lost something much concrete today; my world where you all were involved is going to diminish."

I stand silent as I finished speaking. I can yet see a glimmering drop of tear in her eyes. I don't know exactly how much it means to me; I can't pay much attention to the details as I don't want to turn back now. It's too late to turn back now.

I lift my bag and walk out of the building. I stood there in front of the glass building, just standing and staring at the building.

CHAPTER TWO

I purchased a huge backpack on my way back home, to hold my stuff for my trip to Kasol. It became larger than I predicted however I knew it'd be beneficial withinside the future. I additionally purchased a toiletry bag, eye mask, earphone as I misplaced my iPod and I do not have plenty of time to look for it. The day comes and I pack sufficient garments for two weeks, stroll to the train station. The last time I was this far away from home, I was nonetheless in university. This became definitely my third time going some distance away from home, however each preceding journey has been a single day journey during my time in university and once when I was in school. I had never explored Kasol before, or any place as lovely as it.

I arrive in Kasol and check in at a villa. I chose it because it was really cheap and not very far from the station. I spent the evening on my laptop. My room was small and it was a cold winter evening, so I went to bed around 11 p.m., In the dark, using my cell phone for the light, I quietly unlocked the lock and put keys in the day bag containing my laptop and closed it. I put on my night suit, climbed into the bed, put my wallet, keys and phone under the pillow. I lie down, put on my earphones, put on my eye mask, 'if you can't sleep at a new place, you can at least make your body think you are at home!'

The bedroom has a large window which has been cranked open which gives the cold breeze of the winter wind and also the chirping of the birds.

At 6 a.m., I woke up with a very loud alarm clock. I ignore it for 10 minutes hoping someone will turn it off, but after 10 minutes I'm fully awake. I look around and see my book lying on the study table. I guess I fell asleep while I was reading. However, I am now wide awake so I leave the villa for the day, sleep deprived at 7AM. What a terrible first experience.

I spent the first 4 days going to the Book Cafe, the District Library, the Central Library, The Hosteller. Going library after library, walking back and forth through Kasol, through parks, residential areas, almost getting run over by mad, fast cyclists who run faster than cars. For the first time, I truly understood how beautiful other parts of kasol are

I spent 3 days here trying to make a plan for what I would do next. Eventually I decided to officially retire from work for a while and finish my novel, it wasn't really a decision I had to make, I have already quit my job. But coming to the same conclusion on my own was difficult. I would quit my job, spend a few months recovering, then go backpacking and finish my story. I wasn't quite sure how this would work or if I could do it on my own. The only thing I knew was that I wanted to explore more cities and write more stories. I went into this knowing it was an act of self-destruction, I believe I got what I was looking for.

I found some network near the train station; the internet speed wasn't much but sufficient enough to find a hotel. As my phone got an internet connection my phone was flooded from spam and job application email. There was one notification on Instagram, which was odd as I am not really active on social media, anyway the internet speed was fast enough to check the text and also, I didn't want to check who it was. So, I continued searching for a hotel and found that most hotels were fully booked, but I found a single bed available at a place called Blue Moon, near the Parvati Valley. So, I walked there and checked in. It was getting dark so I went out to get food and sat downstairs in the kitchen area to eat. This is the happiest I have been in 2 years. I sat on the balcony and started reading a book. I came across a very interesting line by Chuck Palahniuk in his novel. I picked my pencil to mark the words

"Only after a disaster can we be resurrected. It's only after you've lost everything that you're free to do anything. Nothing is static, everything is evolving, everything is falling apart."

I lift my phone to check the time, it's 12 at night. Phone screen beeped and I checked there was a new notification from "beats by Blaine"

CHAPTER THREE

I unlocked my phone and went through the notification. Luckily, I have Wi-Fi connection at my room. It's really odd that I received a message request from an unknown or say a known stranger. I went through the profile to make sure who this person is. When I landed on the profile, all I noticed that the person had posted videos from my fav band. And to my surprise I found a short clip of the very song aired by the band. Also, I found the very first version of my favorite music.

I tapped into the video and put on my earphones. As the musician struck the c minor on the piano it made my heart skipped a beat. Maybe this is the magic of music. I laid back to my chair and closed my eyes to feel the depth of the tunes. The cold breeze brushed through my hair, I could feel the moist in the air and the moment I touched my hand I could feel the warmth of the blood running through my veins. My heart had synchronized with the piano tune.

I sat down weaving my dreams and at that moment I realized that it was the right choice, I made. To reach somewhere it's very important to keep the past behind and accept everything and believe in yourself. We cannot change what happened and what might happen. There is no point holding back, we are the creators of our own happiness and our own destruction. it's in our hands.

My eyes started getting heavy, maybe I should sleep now, as I have to go to the cafe library and trust me falling asleep in the library is the last thing that I want to do. I get in my bed, pulled up my blanket and keep my phone aside and close my eyes.

As the morning glorified, I opened my eyes and I could see the ray of sun passing through the window with birds chirping around. I began with my day, starting with a sip of coffee and left for the library. I got back to my room with a few books.

I sat back in the chair and checked on my phone and saw a few messages on Instagram. It was from the same profile.

"Hey there...?", the message reads.

by the time I could process the message another message pops up,

"Your iPod is safe with me".

For a moment I freaked out, how on earth does this person have my iPod. I found it bit creepy, before I could say anything, the message followed,

"Hi this is Malcolm, from the Business Analyst team, The Eve Pvt Ltd".

At this moment I realized we worked at the same place. And the fact that I might have lost the iPod in the office itself.

I locked my phone and kept it aside without replying to any of his texts and continued reading my book.

I took a pause from reading and opened my window. It was late in the evening; I kept my book aside and went outside my room and stepped towards the garden. I always liked roaming around the greens. I enjoyed my evening walk with the view of sunset and dancing through the flowers. It was getting dark so I grabbed my dinner and went back to my room. I checked my phone again, called my mom and took her whereabouts if everything is fine at home. As I disconnected the call, I saw one new unread message from Malcolm. I checked the message,

"I guess you forgot your iPod at your desk while you were leaving, don't worry I kept it safe" his message reads

"I didn't mean to peak into it, but it's good to know that someone really like to listen to my music" he texted again

"BTW I'm Malcolm from the Business analyst department, in case you missed my message". I don't know why but he seems to be a bit annoying. Was everyone in that office annoying or what?

But yet I went to his profile. It is important for me to know who has my iPod I told myself shrugging my shoulders.

Oh, he was born on 06 October he must be a Libra. As I went through his profile, I noticed he really likes black coffee, almost in every photo posted there is one thing common: The Black Coffee. If someone saw my profile all they would find is books.

"If a woman starts investigating, she can leave the CBI behind" I told myself laughing.

"Hey" I texted him back, after a long investigation as I didn't found anything suspicious on him.

"Thanks for keeping my iPod safe"

"That's the least I can do for my fan", he texted back.

"I am just kidding, but it's really nice to know that someone really admires my work". He said

I replied to him with a smiley emoji as I didn't really know how to respond to it and maybe I didn't want to. I kept my phone and started packing my bag as I have to leave for my home. Though the place is beautiful, I can't settle here. I have to get back to my work life.

CHAPTER FOUR

I found myself outside station, inquiring about the train back to Mumbai, in a cold but fresh winter morning. The station was a little overcrowded. It was really hard to not feel intimidated by the sudden pushes people gave in order to get into the train. I made my way to it, until I managed to get inside. Occupied. Occupied. Occupied. And... oh, occupied. I thought as my eyes searched for my seat.

I kept on walking until I found my seat. It was close to the door, but there was a person seating across it. I'd rather sat alone, finding uncomfortable to have a stranger in front of me. However, it was that or remain stand during the thirty hours trip. I shook my head discreetly and sat on my seat, sighing once the train was moved off. From backpack I took out a book which I bought from the library the other day.

After 36 hours of travelling, train finally arrived to my destination. I unpacked my bag, got settled as soon as I reached home. Had a small conversation with my mother and shared all my experience of Kasol and its beauty.

Mom was happy by seeing my face blooming after a very long time. She made my favorite dish for the night. Before going to bed I went through my phone and replied to all the unread messages I had in my inbox.

That night I felt I am finally getting prepared for my new beginning and I can achieve them all.

I set the alarm on my phone, locked it and kept it beside my pillow. The moon had already arrived only to say how beautiful the sun is going to be.

As I woke up to turn off the alarm, there were few messages from Malcolm.

"How are you doing?"

"Let me know when can I hand over your iPod back to you?".

I found his text annoying. I mean of course, I have left the office, now what's the need of being in contact just because of a simple iPod. He must be finding a way to create a conversation. Or he must actually be wanting to return it back.. Well, while being thinking about guys I can always overthink into a different context.

I read the message and left it on seen by just liking it to leave a reply. I got up from my bed, put the phone on charge and began my day with good warm shower. I finished my breakfast followed by drying my hairs. I was at my happiest space today. The room was empty. All I could hear is the silence and my breathing and my hearts beating. I sat on my study table and began writing my personal diary.

I consider my diary as my best friend with no complaints and no demands. Things that I can't share with anyone out there I can share with my diary without even feeling guilty of it. I wrote about Malcolm's text and while writing I remembered about his text and that I should've replied him back for keeping my iPod safe with him.

I got up from my chair, walked towards my bed to get my phone, unlocked it to open Instagram. I texted him back for his efforts.

"Hey, thanks, we shall meet near our office? is that fine with you?", I replied with no such intention of actually meeting him.

To my surprise I got a reply back within a few seconds. Does he always have his phone in his hand or what? I mean whenever I text him, he always replies in an instance.

"Fine, just let me know the date and time, I will be there". - He replied as if he was only waiting for me to text him back asking for a meet.

I wondered for it was strange for me to accept someone's attention and efforts without even asking for it. I am kind of not habituated to such gesture. I mean how on earth a guy could be excited to meet someone? That too me????? When my own guy whom I used to admire the most, dumped me for no reason. Anyways, I replied him.

"17th of march, 5 p.m., is that fine with you?", I replied after checking my schedule.

"Absolutely fine", He replied spontaneously.

He does always have his phone in hand, I laughed.

I am neither excited nor nervous to meet him but I do want to see him. I don't know why, but I did feel like meeting him. After all, he is my favorite musician anyways.

I woke up, got my hair done and worn my newly bought green kurta with rose embroidery on it with addition to rose gold stud earing. I stood in front of the mirror.

"Does it look like I'm over doing it, I mean I am just meeting him to get my iPod back and it's not a date." I thought while I was doing my hair.

"Well, he is my favorite musician. And I got my right to be dressed up." I smiled and picked up my purse and left my house.

While I was waiting for my cab, I checked my watch it was 4:20 and I will reach the venue on time. I always hate being late.

I reached at the decided place on time but he was yet to arrive. I hate when people make me wait.

"Why people can never be on time?" I rolled my eyes asking myself. I kept looking at the road waiting for him to arrive.

It's 5:15 already and I can see everyone leaving from the office. I really don't want my ex-colleagues to find me here. It's not like I hate them but I don't want to face this situation as I haven't even texted or called any of them, not even once.

I was busy biting my nails when I found a guy in a black shirt riding a black bike coming straight towards me. 'Is he Malcolm?', I thought cluelessly. He then turned his bike and parked it.

My eyes met with his light hypnotic brownish eyes that had blaze of sun holding in its iris, he was wearing denim jacket, his hairs was messy but beautiful, his eyes meet mine and he was looking at me with the intensity that can melt the glacier

Is he going for a date straight after handing my iPod or he has dressed up so well just to hand over my iPod back?

I shut of my expression and pretended to be normal as he was standing right in front of me.

"Ha-hey, how are you?", with a clear expression on confusion on his face.

"Hi, I am good, thanks for coming", I replied, not knowing what to say.

"It's ok, don't be so formal, I had to return it anyways", He is trying too hard to be casual.

I smiled.

"He-here's your iPod, trust me, I didn't used it at all, I just unlocked it once to see whom does it belongs to. Hope you didn't mind; I am sorry for that" he said with a nervous smile.

"Never mind, thanks anyways, I have to leave, have some work to finish off" I replied being honest and left.

Indeed, he's cute I mumbled in my mind after taking my iPod back from him.

"Shall I drop you?", He asked.

"Nahh, I am fine, I will go by cab", I answered.

"Alright", he replied dearly raising his eyebrow.

"Btw do you have the access card to the main gate?" He asked mocking with no such intention of actually wanting it while I was walking out of the cafe.

He is that same guy I remembered. He is the one who always annoyed me in the office asking for the access card. The one whom I wanted to punch eagerly I can't believe it's him, but I have to accept it.

I turned back and smiled at him and replied him "No". though he is being cute but yet he is annoying.

I walked out of the café and was waiting for my cab. When I turned to my right, I saw him walking towards me. He walked out of the door and stood beside me. There was clear sign of confusion on my face, not knowing what to say.

He waited along with me until the cab arrived and seen me off biding good bye with a kind smile on his face. As soon as I sat in my cab, I received a text from him.

"Text me once you reach home"

He's so cheesy, I smirked while shaking my head.

"Sure", I replied.

CHAPTER FIVE

I kept the phone inside my bag after replying to his message. I always enjoy my self-space especially while traveling. The trees and the clouds for all intents and purposes make me particularly feel the joyous and gives me peace, which basically is quite significant. But today it is different, I don't know why but after meeting him, a thought kind of hit my mind, maybe I really am just overthinking too pretty much or maybe say the world actually has 30% of population with similar face, his face reminds me of Marvin, generally contrary to popular belief. This could essentially be a coincidence or just me thinking fairly extra ordinarily about Marvin. Maybe I haven't gotten over Marvin yet, or so for the most part thought. The way Malcolm talks to the way he is, his brownish eyes to his cuteness exactly matches to Marvin, demonstrating that this could specifically be a co-incidence

Aahh! Not again, I am not going to think of him or any of them anymore.

I reached at home by 7 p.m. in the evening. Erhhh..!! this traffic got me so late. I stepped inside the room straight as I walked inside of the house. Moma made the coffee and kept it on my study table.

"So late honey? you seem tired, all well?", asked mother.

"Yes mom, nothing much to worry about, I have ample of work", I replied in a pale voice.

I am yet unable to shake his brownish eyes from my brain. Though I tried to ignore, All I could do is end up thinking about him.

I took a deep breath and opened my laptop to write the book I am currently working on. I opened the word file and didn't move the cursor for over 30 mins and I caught myself thinking about how much I loved Marvin. It's been years and yet I can't stop thinking or finding Marvin into everybody I meet. I have to move on...... and I don't know how.

I cannot hold my pen; empty pages have witnessed the thirst of his name. Is it really easy for the person who been in love so passionately to move on? If yes, then what's left in life now?

If given a chance I would definitely let Marvin know how much I really loved him and that he really meant so much to me.

With tears in my eyes and grudge in my heart my hand began writing eventually,

You, my love, have never ever realized
my love, my pain.
I remain lost in the crowd.
Are you still sitting inside me, secretly?
Why are you breaking me mercilessly?
Why can't I replace you?
Whatever I had; I had sacrificed all for you.
You're still alive in me,
I am full of mess,
Left all alone..

I stopped writing as whatever I was writing, it's all about my heart break and how I am ruining myself by overthinking it. I turned off the laptop and closed my eyes breathing the fresh air. The window was open and the moon had arrived. And I realized it's already 9:30 now.

I was so busy thinking about Malcolm and Marvin, I didn't realize the timing. I finished off my dinner on time and got myself comfortable on the bed.

As usual I spent my time in bed scrolling through my Instagram feeds. A new notification popped on my screen. It was Malcolm. I don't know why my heart skipped a beat. I don't know why I am being anxious. To my surprise there were 3 unread messages.

"Did you reach?" the first message reads.

"Hope you reached on time?"

"Heyaaaaaa, there?, hope all well?" before I could type anything another message popped.

"Hey"

"Yeah, I reached on time, sorry, forgot to inform you", I replied, I don't know why but I felt guilty this time. I don't know, was I ignoring him, or was I just lost in my own world. I was so busy thinking of everything that happened today and thinking about Marvin that I forgot to even check my phone.

"I saw your recent posts, there were all beautiful pictures of a beautiful place, the picture would have become more beautiful if it had you in it", He texted being mischievous. I was shocked to know that he wasn't even angry or anything, I mean c'mon I kinda ghosted him.

"Thanks, I had been to Kasol, kinda not a big fan of posting my own pictures on social media", I replied being honest.

"Um, it seems you like travelling a lot, I haven't found any single pictures of you anyhow", he replied.

"hmm" I replied him back and slept without replying to any of his text further. I didn't realize when did my eyes closed and when did the alarm screamed.

After waking up the first thing I did was to check his message.

"I would love to hear the story behind your Kasol trip, I like travelling too, please take me along the next time you plan for such trip"

"?"

"Slept?"

"Good night"

His messages made me smile, even though I didn't reply to him, he doesn't stop texting. Such a kid I thought and caught myself smiling again.

I shook my head a little and kept the phone on charge and went for a good warm shower. The "to do list" was already set for the day. I left for cafeteria by 11 a.m. in the morning itself. When it comes to writing, I don't compromise with time. I have to write a book and launch it no matter what it takes. I must say cafeteria is a best place to read or to write. I began writing as soon as I got settled on the couch of the cafeteria. I ordered mocha cookie Frappuccino and began writing the definition of love according to me,

"I might have fallen to different generation by mistake, where real no longer exist, where love is measured by sacrifice and not by the efforts, where sharing body is more important than sharing emotions. We are all lost in finding love, we are soo lost that we even forgot what it is to be loved. We accept the love that we think we deserve".

I took a pause from writing and had a look on my watch. Has time started moving fast or is it just me too lost with my write ups!? I questioned myself.

Never mind, I shall take a leave now. I left cafeteria by 5:30 p.m. and reached home.

When I reached home, I called Sanika as she is my get away partner and I haven't called her since a long time. I still remember how we used to share our daily tantrums. She is the only friend I have since childhood. While I was talking to her, I thought of sharing about Malcolm but I didn't because I wasn't sure what to say. What exactly I feel.

Laughter and jokes, this is how we end our call which begins with "you know what the fuck happened today?", we are so clingy. Hehehe...,

I cleaned my room after the call, to make it actually look like a room, placed all the books accordingly, made my wardrobe perfectly and finally it was all set and I was all set to scroll my Instagram feeds.

I remembered the messages of Malcolm which I didn't replied to.

"Hey, sorry, yeah, I slept earlier yesterday" I texted him

To my surprise, he was online and replied immediately after seeing my message.

"That's fine fan girl, no need to apologize", said Malcolm.

"Don't tell me you just woke up" followed his next text

"How was your day?", I asked.

"The day hasn't ended yet, anyways, going good", he winked with sarcasm as it was just 6:30 p.m.

";)", I texted as I didn't know what to say but at the same time, I didn't wanted to ignore him

"How's your day going?", his reply came

"Great! I finished the first draft of my book", I said being excited.

"Damn I am so proud of you, I can't wait to read your book", he said.

"Thanks, my friend", I texted. It was odd that I consider him as a friend as I usually don't go out being soo social but this time it is different.

"So how was the trip to Kasol?

"It was good, I was having a tough time recently and I never wanted to be an investment banker, my interest was always about writing, so I took a mini vacation from my daily routine and made writing as my fulltime career", I told him.

"Woah! You're so talented and courageous too, I understand things can get tough sometime and I will try to make sure to get you out of it", he said.

"Hey, I am all well, I am already back to being normal, I am just concentrating into writing now and yeah, one more thing, I may sound talented but not more than you", I said to him not being sure if it was the right thing to say.

"Good to hear that you're back, ahem!, just trying my best to be the best version of myself into music composition. Music always heals" he replied

"Well, what are you doing? "I asked trying to continue the conversation

"Just came home, will finish my dinner then will try to compose something new", he said.

"it's already 11 p.m., you don't sleep or what?" I replied, and even I was shocked to know that it was 11 already.

"Well music is something I love. And I won't even be able to sleep until I have completed the song, don't worry about me, I will sleep by 2-3 a.m., you must sleep now."

"Yaa! Well, all the best, Good night" I replied.

"Good night ;)" his last text for the day

CHAPTER SIX

It had been few of weeks since we met, and to my surprise we had been talking to each other very frequently. We share our goal and dreams and he has to take my tantrums every day. As I was thinking out about our daily conversation his message popped.

"You there on snapchat?"

"Um, I am there but honestly I don't know how to use it, I am a bit social awkward kind of a person", I answered.

"That's fine, anyways, it's not even that necessary to be fully aware of something which is not that essential, don't worry I'm here, I'll teach you." He replied.

"Here's the screenshot of my profile", I replied by sending him the screenshot of the profile of my snapchat id.

He called me up and guided me through the snapchat concept, even though I knew about snapchat I still didn't feel like stopping him. He talked with such a passion and calmness that all I did was just sit back and listen to him.

In the era of ghosting, his name would always appear on the top of my list. It sounds stupid but yeah, we began sharing every small detail of our daily life. Right from what I am going to write to what he's going to compose next. God damn! His passion for music was way beyond words. This person never sleeps! Somewhere his dedication for music became my inspiration for writing. There had been time when we both stayed up late at night, he making his music and me trying to complete my book.

He never missed a chance to motivate me with my write ups.

CHAPTER SEVEN

The sun was about to rise and just like every day I left from my house for morning walk. And for last few days we had been talking to each other on call during our morning walks, and today was no different. We never ran out of topic to talk. I was telling him about the fantasy novel that I was working on. It was about how an angel left heaven and came to earth to find her lost love and how the devils tried to chase her and take her with them.

I was so lost in the story that I didn't even realize that I was alone on the street and when I turned back all I could see is one man who had been following me constantly. I didn't knew what to do, so I started to run, not even waiting to catch my breathe. All I could hear was Malcolm asking me what happened why did you suddenly went quiet and why was I running. I didn't knew what to say. I just told him that noting happed and disconnected the call.

I had been running from my past, running away from the noises and screams but there's nowhere to go. How do I escape my past? The past, the reality chasing, running, never stopping, not even to catch their breath, because your reality is so determined on catching mine. Before you realize the wolves from past haunts you down. Even mornings can turn into nightmare in no time.

It was afternoon I was thinking about what had happened before and what happened today. sometimes the injury heals but the scars remains.

My phone blinked and I unlocked my phone to see a few missed calls and unread messages from Malcolm. I haven't even checked my phone since the morning.

"Hey, you there", his last text reads.

"All good?" he texted again.

"Yeah, I am all good" I replied to him.

"Are you?" he asked

"You sound numb." He texted me, before I can say anything. My phone started to ring. It was him

As I answered the call all he said was "Tell me what's wrong"

"Actually, today while coming back from morning walk, I felt that someone's following me so kind of not feeling well" I told him.

"God, please don't overthink on it, he must might have been there for a walk too. I understand your anxiety, but can I please ask you why do you get anxious on such situations? I don't want to assume anything, could you please tell me, if you don't mind?" he asked. I can feel the concern in his voice. He sounded like he knows what exactly he was saying.

"I haven't really told anyone about this to anyone" I said not knowing what to do.

"It's alright I am here."

"I don't want any sympathy nor I want to be felt sorry for, so let me know if I can really trust you with this" I asked him.

"You can trust me with anything, I never judge, nor I will ever make you feel sympathized." He said calmly.

I told him how I was sexually assaulted by my own uncle when I was hardly a 9-year-old kid and this continued for several year.

"Throughout my life I have only seen how the women of my house has been treated brutally. My moma, sister and my sister-in-law everybody were the victim of domestic violation" I told him. Anyone can easily sense fear in my voice as I speak of it.

"And that's the reason I have dreams. I have dedicated myself to my family and I worked really hard for my sister to get her educated even after being married with two kids and she made it, watching her becoming independent is my biggest dream to make it true before I die" I continued to speak.

After taking a deep breathe I continued "I have never seen a healthy happy married life, my time has shown me the worst part of my life and the only reason I never believe in marriages anymore. In fact, I hate marriage the most. For me, the promise of forever and happily ever after is a myth"

"But then a person walked into my life and changed my thoughts towards men and made me realized not all men who smokes are the monsters and not all men who pray are the saints, Men are beautiful creature of mankind, just because of some bastards I cannot suspect on every man I am around"

"He is a man with morals, ethics and standards and a kind of person worthy to be missed, indeed he was my first love" I have never talked about him with anyone but today I don't know why I just wanted to tell him, tell him everything.

"Things always doesn't work the way we plan for it, I am afraid of getting physically close or say even more afraid that I might get frigid, it was more than anything else that forced me to break up with him, 2 years in a relation madly in love and yet we never had a bed moment & I am happy that he has moved ahead in his life."

"I have been so daunted by everything that I stopped feeling anything. Whatever happened with me back then had left a permanent mark on my life. I feel scared when someone touches me. I haven't felt any sexual attraction. Whenever he tried to come close to me instead of feeling his touch all I felt was fear. I use to feel like someone is grabbing me try to rip me apart, shred me into pieces, I know that was never his intention but my body doesn't respond to touch anymore. Somewhere that incident has broken me, I am broken beyond repair." I paused for a while as this was something I have never shared with anyone

"I can't be normal anymore. My body doesn't respond as it is meant to, my trauma has taken a toll on my sense the only thing I sense is fear." I feel a tear fall from my eyes as I continued speaking.

He kept quiet and listen to every single word of me without interrupting in between. I shared him things that people don't tell to each other for years, not even married couples. I realized how comfortable I am with him and I'm so different around him. These were the things I never even shared with Marvin.

"You're a warrior" he said after a long pause.

"I mean I understand what you might have been through but I believe one day you'll overcome everything and you'll stand strong" the calmness in his voice was giving me the strength that I had been lacking for all these years.

"Thank you! I just need a little space; can we talk later?" I asked him.

"Sure, take care girl" he said before I disconnected the call.

I was expecting his messages tonight but it was left all blank. I did text him another day to which I didn't received any response from him. Every socializing app was left blank and I was eagerly waiting for him to text back. I tried reaching by every possible means. I accepted being ghosted. I mean of course, who would like to be with a woman who is sexually unavailable and messed and broken, Malcolm is definitely not one of those who would be with a woman without expecting sexuality I thought in my mind and that's completely fine. It's absolutely fine to cut people who do not belong to you. But I was wrong. I had not understood him yet.

It's been a few days since he has been ghosting and I had swallowed the anger that I had on him. When he texted me today, he sounded different. He sounded a little numb and I felt upset of thinking that he had been ghosting me for my past. He sounded like something is really going on with him.

"Hey, sorry for texting so late, actually my brother was in ICU and I was really worried about him. It was very unusual; he had never been this sick before. Doctor said, it was due to hypertension, anyways, he's fine now" he said.

"Hey, I am so sorry to hear that, I didn't know about it, are you okay?" I replied trying not to feel guilty.

"Yeah, yeah I am fine, coming days were really tough and I had to be strong but honestly my brother is the only person I have after my parents, I can never imagine losing him" his text reads.

After a long conversation I somehow managed to calm him down. It was surprising to see a guy alike be so caring and emotional. And I remember when he said he had never been like this with anyone. Seems we are both comfortable with each other, we became each other's strength.

CHAPTER EIGHT

Days passed by and we are getting to learn many different things about each other. He's a true fan of Jcole not because of the rap he makes but because of the social fact he raises for societal wellbeing and awareness. Malcolm's idea of loving a personality is way different from others.

He believes on actions and not just words and that's what makes him smart. Bastard with a brain, Kid by heart, matured by sense of humor, that's Malcolm for you. He never misses a chance to make me laugh or ever did he stopped caring for a single minute even at the days when I asked him to leave me alone, he was still there by my side to make me feel that I am not alone. He loves socializing but he trusts carefully and when he trusts there's no going back. He cares carefully but when he stops caring, he won't give a fuck. He's super annoying though. I had become so habituated of him, one day without being annoyed by him made me feel like he's mad at me or maybe he's not well. He's the "Oxymoron":- the most annoying yet the sweetest person of my life. I find him really annoying. Sometimes I hate every stupid word he says, sometimes I want to slap him. There's no one like him, he always keep on getting on my nerves, I know life would suck without him. At the same time, I want to hug him, I want to wrap my hands around his neck he's a jerk but I like him. I had no space for feelings anymore yet his acts were pushing my limits away forcing me to repeat a mistake of falling apart. I ignore what my heart said and dragged my brain towards my passion, my novel, I was trying to write for 3 months.

I continued my book and ghosted him for a week or sometimes just responded with like or memes. My book was almost on the verge of completion. I was overwhelmed with the joy of working harder on my dream. I slept peacefully after realizing the half completion of my book.

My sleep was interrupted by the alarm, anyhow I switch off the alarm and slept back. But after a short time, my phone started to ring again and I thought it was the alarm but when I opened my eye to check the phone and I learned that it wasn't an alarm clock. It's a call from an unknown number. Without thinking much.

"Hello, who is it?", I asked with my sleepy voice.

"Hey, it's me, Akira"- The voice sounded familiar.

I immediately got up from my bed and checked the number again. Suddenly I was wide awake and got my sense back.

"Marvin", I asked after taking a deep breath and sighed.

"Yeah, it's me, Marvin, how are you?" he asked.

"I am good, hope you're going good too" I wasn't sure of what to say.

"Yes, I am good, actually I have called you to invite you on my wedding on 3rd of September 2021, I would like it if you join me on my biggest day"

"Yeah, for sure, may you be blessed in your upcoming journey, Good luck my dearest, take care" I was shocked, I wasn't sure but listening to this somewhere hurt me a little.

I hung up the call after wishing him but did I really mean it? Or it was just my way of holding the grief? I broke down in his memories once again. The love of my life is finally going to move on and here I was holding his memory with solitude trying to move ahead yet I can't. In the principle of love, I am a culprit too, why didn't I die when I lost you. I had no one to share it all except Malcolm, I immediately texted him with tears in my eyes,

"There?"

"Always" he replied

"I have lost everything Malcolm, I lost it, I cannot bear it anymore, please take me away from all of it" I texted him

"Hey, you alright? I am on my way"

"My ex has moved on and I don't know how to deal with this, he had called me in the morning and I don't know how to deal with it after knowing it all"

"I will be there within a while Akira, please don't overthink on it, stop crying first."

He traveled almost 45 Kilometers distance just to meet me. Honestly, the last time somebody traveled for me, covering such a long distance was when Marvin came to end everything with me officially. And why won't he? I wasn't really compatible of the modern-day love.

CHAPTER NINE

It was noon by now and I saw him from the balcony, coming over bike. I ran as fast as I could. The lift was preoccupied so I took the help of staircase and ran 4 floors only to hug him. By the time I reached down there, I saw him having a word with the guard very gently and a bit smile on his face. He was wearing light blue formal shirt and khaki-colored jeans combining with sneakers adding a leather wrist watch which was exactly matching to his cool and wildish personality. I hugged him right at the gate without thinking twice of what would other's think of it. Hugging him felt like a child had got a lost toy. His smile towards my hug made me realized how happy he is to have me in his arms. Isn't it amazing, when you can be completely you around someone without being judged for being whosoever you are? His smile gave meaning to my life. We walked inside the building together and stepped inside the lift.

"Do you have access to the door?" He asked the same annoying question he use to ask in office only to mock me.

"No", I gave him the same old strange angry look.

We both laughed remembering our office days and how I use to hate him at first. I unlocked the door of my house and let him in first. It's 21st century, 'ladies first', criteria had become outdated for me. Men deserve such gesture too. I wanted to do something special for a person who has travelled so long just to stay with me. To my surprise he had got me chocolates, so what if those were the chocolates I skipped eating long back, efforts matter, I laughed thinking about his choice towards chocolates. He's such a nut! I mumbled.

He grabbed me in his arms once again saying, "I didn't get to hug you properly, can I hug you again?". For him a girl's consent was always a priority, be a friend, best friend or a girlfriend and I am not sure what kind of relation I was sharing with him, all I have to say is, 'his hug felt like a poetry'. I was shorter than him so I was covered under his arms and eventually I felt like a new heart beat came up. I got to know I am still alive. There was so much tenacity in the moment, damn I don't have enough words to describe them. My heart asked my breath, if I should die in his arms or should I live a little. Should I kiss the Joys or should I cry a little or live for a while. A hug from a right person can make you forget all your mind's bug. His touch was pure and magical. It was only for me and not for his desire to feel my body but to feel the heart beat and sense my soul. Years of fear vanished within a friction as if I was never afraid of men before. I was so super comfortable with him. I made him visit my house.

I was so messed up since morning that I forgot to clean the room. There were books spread all over the bed with cherry on the cake, laptop opened, earphones and phones messing around. He wasn't surprise though. He was comfortable instead and I offered him to sit on the chair by the time I clean up the room.

"Calm down, its ok, let me know how can I help you" he said looking at my messed-up room.

"Just hold on for 5 minutes, I am done with my stuffs" I replied with a bit of embarrassment.

I cleaned up everything very quickly. He wondered about my passion towards the books, anthologies, poems and literatures.

"How do you read so much? I will sleep before opening the books or I have to carry a whole dictionary along to understand what's written, I am so bad at reading" he said mocking me.

"Just the way you go with music, I go with books" I replied with smile

I offered him coffee and I got one for myself too.

While sipping coffee he took a pack of cigarette out of his pocket. And holding one cigarette in between his teeth he asked, "I hope its alright" to which I nodded. He then lightened it up and took a long drag. I can hear the sound of the burning tabaco and the light that emitted from it lighten up his face a little. After a while he offered me one to which I calmly denied.

He finished the coffee and the cigarette and by the time I came back from the kitchen he had lighten up another cigarette. I laughingly asked him "Is it compulsory for the badass musician to be smoking all the time"

He awkwardly kept the cigarette aside and apologized. I told him that it was alright, I don't really have any problem with it.

By the time we kept talking he got my personal diary which was kept up on the drawer next to him.

"Akira, I guess this is your personal diary, isn't it? He asked without checking what's inside the diary.

"Hell yeah!" I replied, a bit scared as I don't want anyone to read my diary.

"I didn't check it, I have seen you holding it everywhere, so thought of informing you that you forgot to keep it inside your bag" he replied.

I swallowed the breath in peace as I took the diary back from him. I ordered his favorite dishes and asked him to start with the lunch.

"You want to take a snap?" I asked as I know he like taking snaps

"Erh, naahhh! When I had met with the accident badly and I was crippling I use to feel this every moment, why cannot I visit the restaurant and have my favorite food and likewise when I am blessed back to normalcy, I stopped showing off my whereabouts on social media. Yes, I like sharing snaps but not of food or any materialistic stuffs. There would might be many people around who aren't as blessed as I am and they might feel it. One act of immaturity can hurt someone's sentiments and I don't want that for anyone" he replied calmly.

He kept talking continuously about his ups and downs, dreams and nightmares and I kept listening to him like music to ears. For a moment I forgot what happened in the morning and how messed I had been. He shared how did he got closer to his mom during the time he was crippling and that he got to know the real meaning of family. His accident was one of his hardest times for him and that had turned his life.

He says, "I wouldn't have learned humbleness and morals about women's and human's complexity, my mother taught me to respect women and their consent prior to anything else".

He continued talking and I continued melting for his words.

People who know me says, I am the talkative one but with him I was different. I kept listening to him silently. He spoke his hearts out. The real face of a badass was actually an innocent one & there's no need to hate him for being whosoever he is. He is just real. We spoke about our dreams and what we want to achieve in our life. What love means to us.

All of sudden I played the very first version of the music he composed, which was my favorite and due to which we came closer.

"You still have this version with you" he asked out of excitement.

"Yes, I do and I listen to it before going to the bed" I replied with a smile.

Meanwhile I changed my dress at the bathroom to get comfortable. I laid on his chest in my loose t-shirt and pajama with my book and continued reading the left-over part while he was playing with my hair and brushed his hands over my head like a mother pampering a kid. Laying down on his chest felt like, the body burning down in the sun got the shade of a tree. The way he brushed his hands on my head felt like somebody applied some balm on the years of old wound. The kid inside me that died ages ago came back on a little cajoling.

I couldn't concentrate on reading my book because of his cute gesture, all I wanted is to talk to him nonstop and listen him talking continuously.

My life was like a kite with a broken string and today I was here, unsure about tomorrow's morning. Now when a new bond is calling me from behind, why should I get worried about what will happen tomorrow? There's such a prickle in the moment. Now when I have all these with me, I am stuck over, if I should die or live for a while.

I somehow managed reading 1 page and closed the book and we began talking again. He gave a frequent smile and hold my palms into his. I couldn't stop blushing in my mind. I was filled with the mixed feelings. Nervous and excited both at the same time. If I ever get a chance to spend the nights lying on his chest, I would tell the morning not to rise. We were at the closest at the moment. He showed his phone and showed his latest music he is currently working into. Also, his band involved with him into music and how do they practice music at a very calm forester place. Where music meets nature's tune with bird's chirp and open clouds tickling with winds.

I came to know what exactly friendship means to him and that he can go to any extinct to keep his promise and maintain the friendship. He knows how to keep his words. I learned about his best friends, Victor and that they both are together since ages. Another good friend, Ivan, the one who is passionate about rap and poems both. He admires Victor and Ivan a lot.

He respects every relation he makes. He isn't a badass. He is a man with morals, ethics and standards. While he kept showing his photos and videos, I asked him out of context,

"Why don't you let people see good in you?",

"I just want to be me, I don't want to be what people expect me to be." He answered by simply smiling.

"Why don't you mix up with people and go around?" He asked.

Just put your fear down, go out, hang out among friends or companions, meeting and greeting is already written on your destiny, even if you cross a single person on road, that was written for you already, you cannot always run away from your reality. People will scare you only when you decide to get afraid of them, dreams shatter and heart breaks but as long as we have some goodness, the world is still a better place" he added.

“Erh, come on, don’t lecture me, let’s click selfies”, I teased.

We clicked almost 70 pictures together with so many different pose and cherry on the cake he didn’t get bored of it.

They say someday, someone will walk into your life and make you realize why it never worked out with anyone else, with him I felt that. He was that person who walked into my life and made me realize why I never worked out with anyone else.

We checked each and every photo of ours and mocked each other too. He then continued sliding his phone gallery by talking about his family. He swiped to right by narrating about his parents. I saw his parents photos and how politely he was standing with his parents. Trust me this badass becomes an innocent good boy in front of his parents. I laughed. He then swiped right and showed his picture with his elder brother.

The moment I saw his pic with his brother, my mind got traumatized and confused of what to react at the particular moment of time.

“He’s my brother, Marvin, he’s getting married and no excuse you have to attend his wedding” He continued talking and swiping right to left sharing about his bond with him and how close he is to Marvin.

Oceans of thoughts covered my mind dragging me to the darkest mode of mine. For a moment I thought, to tell him the truth about Marvin’s and me. At the same time, I did not want to lose the respect that he has for me in his eyes. It may sound selfish but I really didn’t want to ruin our precious moment. I decided to wait for the right time. When the time is right, I will tell him everything about me and Marvin but not now, I told myself inside my mind.

I went silent and kept faking my smile till the time he was there with me. The coldness in my behavior made him anxious. He did ask if everything's alright with me to which I turned the topic and switched the entire conversation into viewing the sun set from the window. We enjoyed the sunset view. He liked the surrounding around my house and he came up with an idea of going for a trek.

"I really want to go for a trek", he said.

"Go for it!" I replied him with a smile and raising my eyebrow showing joy.

He got himself set to leave my place after the sunset. I didn't want to let him go and asked him to stay a little longer with me. We clicked good bye selfies. By the time he was leaving the house, I asked myself if what should I do and where shall I go? To the left where nothing's right or to the right where nothing's left. I was broken beyond repair yet I managed keeping the smile on my face to not let him get the hint about my dullness. I walked along with him near the parking area to see him off. He held my hands while crossing the road and my heart triggered, "please don't leave me", I didn't showed any of my emotion but I felt each and every hours I spent with him.

"Wanna have a bike ride?", he offered

"Nope dearest, you're already late, you should leave now", I said silently.

"Text me once you're home", I added.

CHAPTER TEN

It's been 3 years without him, I tried moving on but I couldn't. I have got all the fame, recognition and success that I wanted. Indeed, Malcolm is the reason behind my success. He was, he is my inspiration and I will never forget his efforts and the role he played in my life. He has motivated me every time I felt to give up on my dreams. He believed in me when I couldn't believe in myself. He deserves to be written for.

I still remember that day, the day I decided to run away, just because I didn't wanted to spoil his life with my mess. We've gotten too close to each other, telling him the truth would have been difficult or maybe I was too scared of the outcome.

The last time I met him, I only remember, the way I looked at him. It was during Marvin's wedding. I didn't wanted to go the wedding. But I did, only to see Malcolm. The twinkle in his eyes, the curve of his eyebrows, the length of his nose, the perfection of his jaws, the curve of his lips, I watched them approach until his face become blurred and I closed my eyes before I kissed him.

Honestly, I don't want to feel anybody else after him. The book I wrote for him will be released tomorrow. I know he doesn't like reading but I hope someday my books might find a space in his shelf. This is the only way to tell him what I really feel for him and that my vibes with him was for real and not fake. This book is the only way to tell him how sorry I am for being selfish at that time and not letting him know the truth. I will visit Mumbai tomorrow for my book launching ceremony. I remember Malcolm saying, “each person you come across is already written in your stars and you meet everybody for a reason”, this time i will really want to test the destiny. My flight will be on boarded to Mumbai from Delhi by 6.p.m. in the evening and the event at the workshop is at 8 p.m. I hope I meet him if he is in my stars.

CHAPTER ELEVEN

My flight on boarded at Mumbai 10 mins late. I anyhow managed to reach at workshop on time. I attended the launching ceremony and greeted everyone with a smile while my eyes were still looking at the door hoping for him to walk by. Will he really show up today? Would he be knowing that I am in Mumbai? Does he still remember me?

I have made such a huge launch and announcement of this book only to make him aware of it. The clock kept moving, the guests started leaving. I got such a block buster response on this book but it was of no use. The fame, the recognition, the award is nothing without him. What's the benefit of such fame & recognition when you don't have the person you made efforts for? I wasn't surprised but I was numb though. Leaving him was a right choice, how could a person accept someone's present with the darkness of their past? I told myself. Moving away was my decision, staying apart is his choice and I have to accept that.

I opened my personal diary and hold the pen for writing to distract myself from his memory. I was left all alone at the workshop. Everybody left, all I had was silence around me. I wrote and wrote and wrote, all I could write is how he is everything to me but he cannot be the one I want to hold on to.

I closed my eyes for a while and sighed. I took the coffee mug and kept the pen. I looked at the wrist and I learned it's already 12: 15 a.m. It's time to leave, he won't be coming.

There's no use of waiting for him so long. I convinced myself. I took the keys and kept the laptop inside my bag, cleaned my desk too. I walked towards the door and as I turned back to check if I am forgetting something, I heard a voice from outside the door.

"Excuse me, do you have access to the door?"

I closed my eyes and breathed deeply. My stars were asking me to fall apart. I turned back towards the door, adjusted my specs and broke down once again. Should I cry or live a little my heart asked.

He knocked once again and asked,

"Do you have access........."

I opened the door without letting him finish the sentence and answered,

"Yes, I do!" I said with tears in my eyes and smile on my face.

"He's everything he could be but isn't, or maybe he is", my mind mumbled.

Thank you for taking the time to read our stories.
Thank you for being the inspiration.
Thank you for your encouragement and kind words.
Thank you for sharing your points of view, especially when you don't agree.
Thank you for trusting us.

Dear Reader,

Let me ask you something — who is the writer without their readers? It is an eternal question — would art exist without spectator? I don't know the answer. But I know that every time I write — I write with my readers in mind.

Readers are the writer's mirror — in you, we see the reflection of our words and ideas. You help us to shape them, translate thoughts into sentences and communicate them with you.

Knowing that there are people who are genuinely interested in the ideas that we share makes it a whole more interesting. It creates a space for conversation - writing is not a monologue.

It's an indescribable feeling to know that you've touched someone's life, maybe changed it a bit or just gave them a reminder of a thing that they've already known.

Writing makes us friends with the people that we've never met and probably never will. It connects and unites us no matter where we are and who we are.

So thank you, dear reader!

Printed by Libri Plureos GmbH in Hamburg, Germany